# THE ALIEN FILES

## #2 CONSPIRACY

## BY DANIEL COHEN

AN
**APPLE**
PAPERBACK

SCHOLASTIC INC.
New York  Toronto  London  Auckland  Sidney

ISBN 0-590-76342-3

12 11 10 9 8 7 6 5 4 3 2        8 9/9 0 1 2 3/0

Printed in the U.S.A.     40
First Scholastic printing, April 1998

# CONTENTS

THE ALIEN FILES

# CHAPTER ONE

## Origins of a Cover-up

A majority of the American public now believes that the United States government knows *something* about UFOs but is covering up the *truth*.

Surprisingly, surveys show that more people believe that there is a UFO cover-up than believe that there are UFOs. According to a 1997 survey, forty-eight percent of the public believes UFOs are real (thirty-one percent thinks they are imaginary, while twenty-one percent has no opinion). But a whopping seventy-one percent thinks that the U.S. government knows more about UFOs than it is telling us.

The belief that there has been a cover-up — a conspiracy of silence — surrounding UFOs began almost as soon as people began believing in UFOs. And people had good reasons to believe that there was a cover-up.

To understand how this happened, you have to know what America was like half a century ago.

UFOs ("Unidentified Flying Objects" or "flying

saucers," as they were called at first) burst upon our consciousness in mid-1947. World War II had been over for less than two years, and America was gearing up for the Cold War — a long struggle with Russia, or the Soviet Union as it was then called.

The military remained an overwhelming presence in the United States. The country was dotted with military installations, large and small. Many of them were very heavily guarded and very secret. In 1947 America was still very much on a wartime footing.

When people first began to report seeing strange and unidentified objects in the sky, the problem was not turned over to scientists, as it might be today; it was handled by the military, specifically the Air Force. A lot of flying saucer sightings took place near Air Force bases and other military installations, so Air Force control of any investigation seemed natural and inevitable.

The government feared that these objects — whatever they were — might present some sort of danger to the U.S. During World War II Americans had spent years peering anxiously into the sky, expecting an aerial attack from Germany or Japan. By 1947 Americans were scanning the skies once again, this time looking for attackers from Russia.

So having the Air Force take over the investigation of the sightings of strange objects in the sky seemed to be a good idea at the time. However, it turned out to be a very bad idea, creating an aura of suspicion and paranoia about UFOs that persists to this day.

The Air Force officially began to investigate flying saucers in September 1947, just a few months after news of the sightings began to appear regularly in the press. They were genuinely worried about UFOs.

People believed that the disklike crafts were some sort of revolutionary new Soviet aircraft or weapon. At the end of World War II, a lot of German scientists came to America and helped the U.S. develop its missile program. But some German scientists went east to the Soviet Union, and there was a great deal of concern over what sort of weapons they might be developing. Consequently, identifying the sightings was deemed a matter of vital national security. The investigation was under the jurisdiction of Air Force intelligence, at Wright Field near Dayton, Ohio (now Wright-Patterson Air Force Base). It was given the code name Project Sign, though many called it Project Saucer.

Soon the investigators became convinced that flying saucers, whatever they were, did not come from the Soviet Union. Many involved began to believe that the flying saucers might be vehicles from another planet, and during the early months of the project, supporters of the extraterrestrial hypothesis appeared to be in the majority. According to many sources, the Project Sign staff prepared an

"Estimate of the Situation" report in which they supported the extraterrestrial explanation for flying saucers. The report was then sent to General Hoyt S. Vandenberg, Air Force chief of staff.

Just exactly what happened next isn't clear even today, but it is generally believed that General Vandenberg rejected the conclusions because, according to him, there was no solid supporting evidence. The report had been classified "Top Secret," and, after Vandenberg's action, all copies are said to have been destroyed. Project Sign was not off to a good start.

By February 1949 Project Sign was dissolved completely and replaced with Project Grudge. Now those who did not believe that UFOs were extraterrestrial and did believe that they represented no threat to the U.S. were firmly in charge. The stated purpose of Project Grudge was to do as little as possible, wind up current investigations, reassure the public that everything was under control, and then go out of business — assuming that the flying saucer hysteria would simply die down.

Project Grudge did not go as the Air Force had planned. In the first place, at least some of the witnesses who reported seeing flying saucers or UFOs were actually seeing secret military devices. Classified high-altitude balloons were responsible for some of the most well-publicized and sensational reports of the time. But since the balloons were secret, Air Force investigators couldn't talk about them. They made up explanations that to the public were clumsy and obvious lies.

A second problem was that the investigators were not scientists. Though they had a little scientific help, the investigators were on their own most of the time. In their attempt to explain every single sighting as the result of misidentification of natural phenomena such as a meteor, a planet, or a flock of birds, they made a series of horrendous scientific mistakes.

They also looked as if they were trying to intimidate witnesses. Immediately after a sighting, Air Force investigators began looking into the backgrounds of the witnesses to see if the witnesses were reliable. They routinely checked police and FBI files and interviewed witnesses' friends, fellow employees, and acquaintances. Small wonder that many of those who innocently reported that they had seen a strange light or object in the sky began to feel they were being harassed or were suddenly under official suspicion. The investigators scared people and made them angry.

The public began to wonder if the Air Force investigators were simply incompetent, or whether — a more sinister explanation — they were engaged in a massive cover-up. The phony explanations and mistreatment of people whose only crime was that they had seen something strange in the sky looked downright un-American.

Adding to the growing belief in an official cover-up was the military passion for discipline, order, and confidentiality. Air Force investigators couldn't talk freely about their investigations. There were very strict regulations about how information about UFOs could be made public. The most important was AFR (Air Force Regulation) 200-2, or "the notorious AFR 200-2," as it was always called by UFO buffs.

According to the regulation, information gathered on a UFO sighting had to be submitted to Washington first and could only be released by the Secretary of the Air Force. There was only one exception:

"Information regarding a sighting may be released to the press or the general public by the commander of an Air Force base concerned only if it has been *positively identified as a familiar known object* [italics in the original] . . . if the sighting is unexplainable or difficult to identify, because of insufficient information or inconsistencies, the only statement to be released is the fact that the sighting is being investigated and that information about it will be released at a later date."

The regulation also stressed the importance of reducing the number of unidentifieds to a minimum. "If more immediate, detailed, objective data had been available, probably those too would have been explained."

In short, if you can't explain it away, you'd better not talk about it.

Heavy penalties were threatened for those who disobeyed AFR 200-2, though there is no evidence that anyone was ever punished for disobeying the regulation.

The Air Force tried hard to control what appeared in the press. At first, the press did not treat the subject of flying saucers very seriously. Most reports on sightings were sensationalized, inaccurate, and regarded as jokes. But accounts of flying saucer sightings kept coming, and often the reports came from people such as airline pilots who were considered responsible witnesses. So the press began taking the subject more seriously.

Air Force investigators were generally uncooperative with reporters. As a result, it was the investigators, rather than the witnesses, who were taking a beating in the press. They were being portrayed as incompetent, evasive, and worse. The Air Force felt that it needed to counterattack. At that time, one of the most widely read and influential publications in America was the magazine *The Saturday Evening Post*. The Air Force selectively granted permission to *Post* writer Sidney Shallet to do a two-part article on the subject of flying saucers. But they wanted to make sure that the article would present interest in flying saucers as a nonsensical waste of time. They only showed him information that would play down UFOs. The article contained phrases like "the great flying saucer scare" and "rich, full-blown screwiness." The articles appeared in April and May 1949 but seem to have had the opposite of the intended effect on public opinion, because within a few days of publication reports of flying saucer sightings reached a new high.

Far more influential was an article that appeared in the January 1950 issue of *True* magazine. It was called "Flying Saucers Are Real." The author was retired Marine major Donald E. Keyhoe. Keyhoe had been an aircraft and balloon pilot during World War II and had an established reputation as an aviation journalist. He had lots of contacts in the military and aviation communities.

After some months of research, Keyhoe had come to the conclusion that flying saucers were vehicles from other planets that were keeping the earth under surveillance. He effectively demolished some of the Air Force explanations of well-publicized sightings. The extraterrestrial explanation wasn't new, but the article stressed that the Air Force already knew a great deal about spaceships and was covering up their information. The article had a tremendous impact and resulted in the largest sale of any issue of *True*, a fact not lost on other publishers. Keyhoe was widely interviewed by newspapers, on radio, and on television.

Keyhoe went on to write a series of popular books, including *The Flying Saucer Conspiracy* and *Flying Saucers From Outer Space*. More significantly, he went on to become head of the National Investigation Committee on Aerial Phenomena (NICAP), by far the largest and most influential of all the UFO groups. Because of his background, Keyhoe was able to attract a fairly high-powered board of governors for his organization. It was heavily weighted toward military men and included people like Vice Admiral Roscoe H. Hillenkoetter, who had been appointed by President Harry Truman to be the first head of the fledgling Central Intelligence Agency. Hillenkoetter joined NICAP after he retired from government service.

In a policy statement, the NICAP board of governors said:

"The Air Force has withheld and is still withholding information on UFOs; NICAP intends to secure all verified factual evidence and make it available to Congress and the public."

Keyhoe was convinced that there was a great behind-the-scenes struggle taking place in the Air Force and some of the government security agencies between those who wanted to shoot down or capture alien spaceships and those who wanted to try to communicate with them peacefully.

For Keyhoe and for NICAP, the cover-up became a much bigger issue than the alien ships themselves. Because of their influence, the cover-up became a major, if not *the* major, part of the UFO story. It remains so today.

Why was the U.S. government, and indeed most of the governments of the world, so determined to cover up all information about UFOs as alien spaceships? Keyhoe and his supporters said it was fear of panic.

No one could discuss the subject of the UFO cover-up for long without mentioning the famous Orson Welles *The War of the Worlds* broadcast in 1938. The actor's realistic dramatization of the H.G. Wells "invasion from Mars" novel created a small but genuine panic. What would happen if the public discovered that Earth really was being visited by space aliens? There would be mass hysteria, governments would collapse, and the world would fall into anarchy — not the best state in which to deal with alien contact. People reasoned that the government was trying to cover up the truth until it had developed some strategy for dealing with the contact.

Keyhoe was much more optimistic about the public's ability to deal with such a revelation: "Today we are already living with the constant danger of surprise nuclear attack by an enemy nation. We know that such an attack could kill millions of people and destroy much of civilization. Yet we do not live in overwhelming fear.

"Whatever the answer to UFO aliens may be, we

would not be utterly paralyzed. The American people have proved they can take shocking situations . . . without collapsing in fear. If prepared carefully — and honestly — they can take the hidden UFO facts, startling as they may be."

The most dramatic point in the dispute between Keyhoe and the Air Force came in February 1958. A popular TV program called *Armstrong Circle Theater* was presenting a one-hour show on UFOs. Keyhoe was among the guests scheduled to appear. Like most TV shows in those days, it was shot live. Keyhoe had reluctantly agreed to read from a prepared script. But with the cameras on him, he abandoned the script to attack the Air Force cover-up. The audience at home never heard him, for the moment he departed from the script the producers turned his sound down — all you could hear was a faint murmur. But you could see Keyhoe's tense, angry face delivering what looked to be a significant statement. Many viewers thought that something had gone wrong with their TV sets; then they realized that Major Keyhoe had been silenced.

The Air Force had nothing to do with the silencing. The producers didn't know what Keyhoe was going to say, and with visions of libel suits passing before their eyes, they cut his sound. In 1958 what could be said on TV on any subject, including UFOs, was far more restricted than it is today.

The initial Air Force reaction was to deplore what the TV producers had done, because they felt that silencing Keyhoe had given his charges added publicity. Later, they seemed to conclude that they really hadn't suffered because Keyhoe made himself look bad by departing from the script. The whole time, the Air Force continued to hope that the UFO problem would go away.

The primary agent of the cover-up was assumed to be the Air Force. But gradually the focus shifted to the increasingly powerful secret agency, the Central Intelligence Agency (CIA). The elevation of the CIA to chief conspirator came despite the fact that former CIA chief administrator Hillenkoetter was an official of NICAP. This led some UFO buffs to conclude that NICAP itself was a CIA front organization and part of the conspiracy of silence.

In fact the CIA did become involved in UFO investigations in 1952. At the request of the White House, the CIA appointed a panel of distinguished scientists, headed by California Institute of Technology physicist Dr. H.P. Robinson, to look into the subject. Dr. Robinson demanded access to all top-secret military data that might have a bearing on UFOs. After some serious discussions, the Robinson panel concluded that UFOs presented no direct threat to U.S. security, but worried that the military would confuse a UFO with a rocket attack from the Soviet Union. The panel also noted that five to ten percent of the UFO reports were highly reliable and had not been adequately explained.

Keyhoe, however, was convinced that CIA involvement was much deeper than that. His organization had been actively promoting the gospel of a government cover-up for years. Additionally, a number of influential congressmen, including Senator Barry Goldwater of Arizona, had told him that they had been denied access to secret UFO information.

NICAP was planning an attack on UFO secrecy. The main part of the plan was to be a big press conference featuring several new UFO witnesses and chaired by ex-CIA head Vice Admiral Hillenkoetter. He was going to repeat, in public, his conviction that UFOs were under intelligent control and that the government was covering up this fact. It was an event that would have had a real impact. But it never happened.

As soon as plans for the press conference began to take shape, some who were supposed to take part in the event reported being harassed and threatened by CIA agents. The crushing blow came when Hillenkoetter abruptly resigned from NICAP.

His letter of resignation read in part: "In my opinion, NICAP's investigation has gone as far as possible. I know the UFOs are not U.S. or Soviet devices. All we can do now is wait for some action by the UFOs.

"The Air Force cannot do any more under the circumstances. It has been a difficult assignment for them, and I believe we should not continue to criticize their investigations."

Keyhoe was astonished. He had known Hillenkoetter for years, and the vice admiral had always been convinced that the cover-up had to be exposed. Now on the eve of what would have been a very important event, he reversed his opinion.

Keyhoe said that the only possible reason for this reversal was "persuasion at a very high level that it was his duty to help block a showdown."

The press conference that was supposed to crack the cover-up was never held. But the idea of a cover-up survived, thrived, and today is more firmly planted in public consciousness than it ever was.

# CHAPTER TWO

## The Air Force Bails Out

After Project Grudge came Project Blue Book, the longest-lived and best-known of the Air Force attempts to investigate and, according to some, cover up UFOs.

By 1950 the initial Air Force attempts to investigate and explain UFOs had practically disappeared. But the UFOs had not. There were more sightings of mysterious objects in the sky and more interest in the subject than ever before. Ridicule hadn't stopped reports of UFOs. So, in 1951, the Air Force decided that they had better start investigating the subject again — or at least look as if they were investigating the subject. Project Blue Book was born.

The first director of Project Blue Book was Captain Edward J. Ruppelt, a veteran combat pilot with a degree in aeronautical engineering. Captain Ruppelt took his job very seriously. He and his small staff tried to investigate the UFO sightings that were reported to them. All too often Blue

Book investigators were hampered, not by official secrecy, but by a lack of resources and the fact that UFO investigation was very low on the Air Force list of priorities. When there was a major UFO sighting Ruppelt sometimes read about it in the newspapers first.

Ruppelt was head of Project Blue Book for two years. After he retired he wrote a book called *The Report on Unidentified Flying Objects*, published in 1956. The book was a remarkably candid account of the Air Force investigation. Though not a best-seller like some more sensational UFO books, it became a classic among serious UFO buffs.

Ruppelt couldn't reveal all of the UFO information he knew. For example, in the case of one highly publicized sighting he concluded that the lights had been "positively identified as a very commonplace and easily explainable natural phenomenon."

However, Ruppelt couldn't tell the reader what the natural phenomenon was or how that conclusion had been arrived at. "It is very unfortunate that I can't divulge the exact way the answer was found because it was an interesting story of how a scientist set up a complete instrumentation to track down the lights and how he spent several months testing his theory until he hit upon the answer. Telling the story would lead to his identity, and in exchange for his story, I promised the man complete anonymity. But he fully convinced me that he had the answer, and after having heard hundreds of explanations of UFOs, I don't convince easily."

Ruppelt did explain in detail how some other sightings had been identified and frankly admitted that some cases could not be explained. He often expressed frustration over the lack of cooperation he received from his superiors in his investigations.

His conclusion was remarkably open-minded: "I wouldn't hazard a guess as to what the final outcome of the UFO investigation will be. . . . Maybe the final proven answer will be that all of the UFOs that have been reported are merely misidentified known objects. Or maybe the many pilots, radar specialists, generals, industrialists, scientists, and the man on the street who have told me, 'I wouldn't have believed it either if I hadn't seen it myself,' knew what they were talking about. Maybe the earth is being visited by interplanetary spaceships. Only time will tell."

Ruppelt, the man who headed the Air Force investigation of UFOs during its most active period, had very much left open the possibility of extraterrestrial visitors.

Three years after the original book appeared, Ruppelt put out a second edition with three additional chapters. In these new chapters he appeared to back away considerably from this point of view and drew more negative conclusions about the possibility of extraterrestrial visitors. Many in the community of ufologists suspected that he had been pressured to change the book. We shall never know, because Captain Ruppelt died a few months after the publication of the revised edition of the book.

However, later in the 1960s when a paperback edition of Ruppelt's book was published, it was the original book, not the more negative revision, that was reprinted.

After Ruppelt's departure, Project Blue Book ran steadily downhill. The staff was reduced to a major, a sergeant, and a couple of secretaries. An outside consultant was brought in every once in a while when absolutely necessary. Blue Book clearly didn't have the resources or staff to conduct investigations, even if it had wanted to. Air Force brass were fully convinced that UFOs presented no threat to the United States and that what people were reporting were misidentifications of ordinary things. Project Blue Book became a holding operation, a public relations front, a way for the Air Force to say that, yes, indeed, it was investigating these sightings that so fascinated the public, without actually doing much of anything.

Investigations were increasingly being carried out by various civilian UFO groups — almost always groups of people who already believed that UFOs were spaceships, such as NICAP and the Aerial Phenomena Research Organization (APRO). The civilian organizations also kept up a drumbeat of criticism of the Air Force, either for conducting an inadequate investigation or for actually covering up the truth. For the Air Force it was a no-win situation. They desperately wanted to get out of the UFO business but didn't know how. Interest in the subject never faded away as so many had predicted it would.

In 1966 there was a well-publicized wave of UFO sightings in Michigan. Voices were being raised in Congress for a more thorough investigation of the subject of UFOs. One of the loudest voices was that of Congressman Gerald Ford. Ford was later to become president of the United States after the resignation of President Richard Nixon. In 1966 he was a congressman from Michigan and House minority leader.

Some congressional hearings were held, but they didn't amount to much. At the hearings Dr. J. Allen Hynek, longtime scientific adviser to Project Blue Book, first publicly expressed his dissatisfaction with the Air Force investigation. It was finally decided to put the whole investigation into the hands of a specially chosen scientific panel. Congress was extremely pleased to pass this potentially embarrassing hot potato on to someone else.

The federal government appropriated some $300,000 for a UFO study. But no one would touch the job. It is very unusual to find a large grant that no one wants to take. But most scientists regarded the study of UFOs as unworthy of their time and as potentially dangerous to their careers.

They feared being labeled as fringe scientists. Simply to undertake such a study took courage. It also meant getting mixed up in what had become a highly emotional and very public subject.

After being turned down by several of the most prestigious universities in the country, the Air Force finally persuaded the University of Colorado to undertake the task. The project head was Dr. Edward U. Condon, a distinguished physicist with an international reputation. He was so well established that he could not be easily harmed by an association with UFOs.

Condon had another desirable quality. He was used to the rough-and-tumble of public controversy. Back in the 1950s he was one of a number of scientists accused of being a security risk. Condon's chief accuser was an ambitious young politician from California named Richard Nixon, who later became president of the United States.

Condon refused to take the accusations lying down. He brought his case before a variety of review boards — and was ultimately vindicated. Even to undertake such a fight against so formidable a foe as Nixon took courage, and victories like Condon's took tenacity as well. He was going to need both to head the UFO study.

At first Condon didn't really want the job. He had no previous interest in UFOs. But he was finally flattered and cajoled into heading the committee.

Condon's appointment was announced on October 7, 1966, and there were public expressions of joy and relief. Dr. Hynek said he felt vindicated, and Keyhoe was delighted. But from the very beginning there were rumblings of discontent about the Condon Committee.

The committee staff itself was divided between pro-UFO people — those who already believed that UFOs were spaceships — and anti-UFO people — those who believed that it was all hoax, mistake, and misinterpretation. The anti-UFO forces were in the majority and the pro-UFO forces soon became disillusioned by what they felt to be Condon's negative and unserious attitude.

A war within the committee broke out when one pro-UFO staff member found a memorandum written by project coordinator Robert Low, which seemed to indicate that the whole study was little more than a public relations gimmick; that the scientists involved really had no hope at all of finding anything significant.

"The trick would be to describe the project so that, to the public, it would appear a totally objective study, but to the scientific community, would present the image of a group of nonbelievers trying their best to be objective, but having almost zero expectation of finding a saucer." In short, Low thought it would be important to tip off other scientists to the fact that the committee wasn't made up of a bunch of saucer-chasing nuts. He thought the best way to accomplish this end was to stress the "psychology and sociology of persons and groups who report seeing UFOs."

The memorandum was shown to Keyhoe and leaked to the press. The result was an explosion of protest from pro-UFO people and an explosion of anger from Dr. Condon. He promptly fired the two men accused of leaking the memo.

If there had ever been a hope that the Condon Committee was going to convince the public that UFOs were not spaceships, that hope was blown away in the resulting controversy. *Look*, one of the largest-circulation magazines of the day, ran an article entitled "Flying Saucer Fiasco." The article said that the Condon Committee could never find alien spaceships, because it was committed to not finding them.

Condon became increasingly grumpy and short-tempered. He traded threats of libel suits with some of his critics.

The general public always thought that scientific controversy was a polite and scholarly affair and that scientific questions could be solved by an objective study of the facts. But now they were both entertained and confused by this kicking, eye-gouging street fight among PhDs. Congress even got back into the act by holding some inconclusive hearings.

The Condon Committee's final report was made public early in January 1969. It was a bulky

1,500-page collection of papers on a variety of subjects written by staff members and hired consultants. A total of ninety-one UFO cases of different types had been analyzed in depth. In slightly better than two-thirds of the cases, the committee felt it had been able to identify the origin of the UFO. This left one-third of the cases unidentified.

Anti-UFO people said the percentage of unidentified cases was not extremely high, because even in the best of cases data were incomplete and 100 percent identification would be impossible. Pro-UFO people said that the one-third of the unidentified cases proved that there were genuine UFOs.

In his introduction, Condon concluded that there was absolutely no evidence to indicate that Earth was being visited by extraterrestrial spaceships. He claimed that nothing useful could be learned from any further study of the subject. It would be a waste of time and money.

In general the report was warmly received by the scientific community. But the general public had already discounted it because of the controversy. Although 100,000 paperback copies of the Condon Report were issued with considerable fanfare, most of the copies went unsold. Today only an exceptionally well-stocked library will possess a copy of what was supposed to be the final word on the UFO controversy. Polls showed that the public's attitude toward UFOs and cover-ups had not changed a bit.

The Air Force used the Condon Report, widely doubted or not, as an excuse to finally get out of the UFO business. The report had recommended ending Project Blue Book, and the Air Force did exactly that. There were few tears shed at its funeral. The Blue Book files were shipped to Maxwell Air Force Base in Alabama, where anyone could look at them. Some people did, but found they contained no great secrets or revelations.

Of course, those who had believed in a cover-up insisted that the Blue Book files had already been carefully purged of all significant information.

After the release of the Condon Report and the end of Project Blue Book, *Time* magazine ran an article headlined "Saucers End."

Now, thirty years later, the response to that headline must be "no way."

# CHAPTER THREE

## The Majestic Twelve

In the enormously popular 1996 film *Independence Day*, there is a scene in which the President of the United States is taken to a secret laboratory. There he is shown the remains of a UFO that had crashed nearly a half century earlier and the alien creature that had been in it. The President is surprised, because this laboratory and the whole UFO project had been kept secret from him.

The film was science fiction, but it raises an interesting question. Would it have been possible for some agency like the CIA or a super-secret "silence group" within the government to keep startling UFO information hidden from a series of presidents?

Back in the late 1940s and early 1950s, a lot of UFO buffs believed that it was indeed possible. But as time went on that theory began to seem less and less likely. If something as big as confirmed contact with space aliens was being covered up, then the President — all the presidents — must have known about it right from the start.

That belief seemed to have been spectacularly confirmed by the sudden appearance in 1984 of what came to be called the Majestic Twelve documents.

In December of that year a plain brown envelope arrived at the North Hollywood home of documentary filmmaker Jaime Shandera. The envelope had an Albuquerque, New Mexico, postmark but no return address or any other clue as to the sender. Inside the envelope was a roll of 35mm film.

When developed, the film turned out to contain what appeared to be parts of several official government papers from the earliest days of the flying saucer era.

Shandera was not a well-known UFO researcher, but he had worked with the writer William Moore. Moore was coauthor of a book called *The Roswell Incident,* which had helped to propel the belief in a crash of a flying saucer near Roswell, New Mexico, in July 1947 from an obscure piece of flying saucer lore to the most celebrated UFO case in history. Why the information was sent to the unknown Shandera — rather than to Moore himself, or any one of a score of others in the UFO field — is unclear, but it is just one of many things about the documents that is unclear.

Shandera gave the material to Moore, who did nothing with it for over two years. The documents didn't become public knowledge until a British author released some of them to a London newspaper in 1987.

A controversy over who leaked what to whom, and when, raged in the world of ufologists. But as far as the public was concerned, that was just a sideshow. What people really wanted to know was what the documents contained.

The earliest of the documents is supposed to be a memorandum dated September 24, 1947, written on White House stationery to Secretary of Defense James Forrestal and signed by President Harry Truman. It was about setting up an "undertaking . . . that shall be referred to only as Operation Majestic Twelve." Later in the memo the reference is shortened to MJ-12.

"It continues to be my feeling," the memorandum concludes, "that any future considerations relative to the ultimate disposition of this matter should rest solely with the Office of the President following appropriate discussions with yourself, Dr. Bush, and the Director of Central Intelligence."

Clearly the operation was supposed to be secret. But what was it?

That was made clear in the second top-secret document, a briefing document of five pages, four of them typed single-spaced, prepared for President-elect Dwight D. Eisenhower on November 18, 1952, by Vice Admiral Roscoe Hillenkoetter, CIA chief and MJ-1, number one of the Majestic Twelve.

The brief began with a review of the earliest flying saucer sightings, concluding, "Public reaction bordered on near hysteria at times."

Then the document went on to explain how a UFO crashed near Roswell, New Mexico, in July 1947. The most sensational part of the document read:

"On 07 July 1947 a secret operation was begun to assure recovery of the wreckage of this object for scientific study. During the course of this operation, aerial reconnaissance discovered that four small, humanlike beings had apparently ejected from the craft at some point before it exploded. These had fallen to Earth about two miles (three kilometers) east of the wreckage site. All four were dead and badly decomposed due to action by predators and exposure to the elements during the approximately one week that had elapsed before their discovery.

"A special scientific team took charge of removing these bodies for study. The wreckage of the craft was also removed to several different locations. Civilian and military witnesses in the area were debriefed and news reporters were given the effective cover story that the object had been a misguided weather research balloon."

The story told in the document follows the basic line of the book on Roswell that Moore coauthored, though there are several significant variations in detail.

By November 1947, the briefing document concludes, a team of government scientists had realized that "although these creatures were humanlike in appearance, the biological and evolutionary processes responsible for their development had been quite different from those observed or postulated in Homo sapiens."

It was suggested that the beings should be referred to as Extraterrestrial Biological Entities, or EBEs.

Detailed information about the crashed flying saucer (thought to be a short-range reconnaissance craft), about a form of writing found in the wreckage, about the studies of the EBEs' bodies, even about the exact details of the recovery and disposition of the materials found at the crash site were to be provided in a series of attachments, A through H. Unfortunately only attachment A, the Truman letter, was included in the material sent to Shandera. A great wealth of potentially fascinating material was simply missing. What was left was little more than an outline, with few details to be checked.

There was, however, one detail that engaged the attention of a lot of people. That was the list of the Majestic Twelve — the twelve eminent men who were supposed to be overseeing this enormous investigation and cover-up.

One of the names on the original list was Secretary of Defense James Forrestal. But a footnote added that Secretary Forrestal died on May 22, 1949. He committed suicide. His place on the committee was later taken by General Walter B. Smith.

The names of several other military men appeared on the list. Right at the top, MJ-1 was Vice Admiral Roscoe H. Hillenkoetter, first head of the CIA and onetime board member of the pro-UFO organization NICAP. Some ufologists had always suspected that the old CIA man was really a double agent bent on hindering rather than helping NICAP's search for the truth.

Generals Nathan Twining, Hoyt Vandenberg, and Robert Montage were on the list, as were several leading scientists, such as Drs. Vannevar Bush, Detlev Bronk, and Lloyd Berkner — but surely the most surprising name among the twelve was that of Harvard astronomer Dr. Donald Menzel.

Menzel was well known to ufologists as one of the earliest, most ferocious, and most tenacious debunkers of UFOs. He had said repeatedly that the whole extraterrestrial idea was absolute nonsense. Yet here he was being listed as one of the chief architects of a massive cover-up of a spaceship crash — a notion that he had denounced and ridiculed so often. To many of those who had locked horns with Menzel over UFOs, the idea that the Harvard astronomer could actually have known about a crashed spaceship with aliens aboard and thus had been living a lie for over twenty years seemed incredible, unbelievable. Yet if the MJ-12 document was at all credible, that would have been the case.

Menzel, like Hillenkoetter and all the others on the list, was long dead by the time the MJ-12 documents surfaced and thus unable to confirm or deny the story.

UFO writer and lecturer Stanton Freedman says he has found evidence that Menzel was indeed leading a double life when it came to UFOs. "People of that era," Freedman says (that is, people who did classified work during World War II), "knew how to keep secrets."

Menzel's friends and associates regarded such speculation as utter nonsense. Said Dr. Ernest Taves, who had worked closely with Menzel for years, "I state categorically that he [Menzel] would have repudiated with contempt any suggestion that he participate in the cover-up proposed in the alleged secret document."

While the MJ-12 documents looked authentic, there was no way to prove that they were. No one knew where they came from. Since they were only photographs, there was no way of testing the paper and ink to see if they really were documents prepared in the late 1940s or early 1950s. They could have been faked.

Then Moore and Shandera released a third document. This was not a photograph. According to Moore, they had found this document among President Eisenhower's official papers stored in the Eisenhower Library. It is a July 14, 1954, memorandum from Robert Cutler, special assistant to the President, to General Nathan Twining, regarding a change of time for the meeting of the MJ-12 group on July 16. It gives no hint as to what MJ-12 is, but it is the only documentary support, aside from the photographs sent to Shandera in 1984, that a group with that code name existed at all.

All of the MJ-12 documents were finally released to the press on May 29, 1987. They captured more attention than any other UFO story had for many years. Generally respectful accounts appeared in *The New York Times*, *The Washington Post*, and a host of lesser-known papers throughout the world. But heightened publicity brings heightened scrutiny and criticism. For example, Robert Cutler, the author of the memo, was out of the country on the date the memorandum was supposed to have been written and therefore could not possibly have written it.

What was found amid the Eisenhower papers was supposed to be a carbon copy of the original memo, but it was not on the official government onionskin paper that was used for copies of all memos and other official documents in 1954. It had the wrong classification numbers and appeared to have been typed on the wrong sort of typewriter.

The discovery of the memo was also suspicious.

It was in a box of documents that had recently been declassified and opened to the public — one of hundreds of similar boxes of documents that had been declassified. The amount of information classified as secret in Washington is staggering, and these Eisenhower documents were, by and large, routine and uninteresting. Out of the numerous boxes, it is strange that Moore and Shandera picked that one. Rumors circulated that they had been "tipped off." It is also quite possible that they carried a phony document with them and claimed that they found it in the box.

Two other possibilities have been widely discussed. First, that the documents were being deliberately leaked by the government in order to prepare the public for the eventual revelation of the truth about UFOs. If public reaction is unfavorable, the government can always deny that the documents are genuine.

Alternately, the documents may be fakes deliberately planted by the government as part of a disinformation campaign to confuse and discredit UFO researchers.

Take your pick of explanations.

A year or so after the MJ-12 story became public, a videotape was circulated throughout the ufological community. It was supposed to be an interview with an Air Force intelligence officer codenamed "Falcon."

Falcon said that Earth had been visited by representatives of nine different alien races. The one he talked about most was composed of little gray-skinned people who came from the third planet in the system of Zeta Reticuli. They had been here for 25,000 years and had profoundly influenced human evolution and religion.

Falcon discussed the Majestic Twelve and something called Project Aquarius, the umbrella operation for all the cover-ups and extraterrestrial contacts. Unfortunately, no one who saw the tape would be able to recognize Falcon if they met him. His face was always in the shadows, and his voice had been electronically altered. All of the mystery leads one to believe that Shandera most likely made the tape.

Moore insisted that he was not trying to be deliberately mysterious about Falcon's identity but that there were confidences that had to be respected. "If I didn't, these people wouldn't talk to me in the future," he said. He also promised new and startling revelations — "soon."

That was back in 1988. A decade later we are still waiting for the revelations.

# CHAPTER FOUR

The Presidential Flying Saucer

We have already discussed how unlikely it would have been for a massive cover-up of the truth about extraterrestrial visitation to have been carried out without the involvement of the President of the United States.

In fact, the names of several U.S. presidents of the last half century have been closely associated with UFOs. The modern age of flying saucers began in 1947 when Harry S Truman was in the White House.

In the 1980s Truman was associated with establishing the super-secret Majestic Twelve to coordinate the UFO cover-up. In the 1990s Truman has been mentioned in reference to UFOs and occasionally even been portrayed by an actor in TV shows about UFOs. But in the 1940s and early 1950s when he was president, Truman never said anything publicly about the subject.

In those early days, the idea of a cover-up was associated almost exclusively with the Air Force.

The Roswell story got a brief burst of publicity in July 1947. Then the Air Force said that what had crashed at Roswell was just an ordinary weather balloon, and most people believed them at the time. Even people who thought flying saucers really were spaceships from another world forgot about Roswell for years.

At first people assumed that the cover-up could be carried out at a fairly low level, or by a secret "silence group" within the government, without the knowledge of the president or other high officials.

But by the early 1950s, people believed that the cover-up, if there was one, had to be huge. There had been too many sightings, too much publicity. Any cover-up this extensive couldn't be the work of a few nervous Air Force officers — the president had to know. For that reason the president whose name is most frequently linked to UFOs is Truman's successor, Dwight D. Eisenhower, or "Ike" as he was affectionately called.

Before he became president, Eisenhower had been a general in the army. At the time, UFO buffs figured that Ike, with his military background, would have been acutely sensitive to a military cover-up. He couldn't have been fooled.

Certainly the most famous incident in the rumored underground association of President Eisenhower and flying saucers came on February 20, 1954. The President was on a golfing vacation in

Palm Springs, California. A president is never truly alone or out of view of the press corps for very long, but on February 20, President Eisenhower apparently disappeared from the ranch where he was staying as a guest.

Wild rumors began to circulate. Today, every detail of a president's health is front-page news. But in 1954 much was kept from the public. The Washington press corps knew, though the public did not, that President Eisenhower was not in robust health. Indeed, the following year he suffered a nearly fatal heart attack. So when he dropped from sight, some immediately thought that a medical emergency had occurred. In fact, one report was that he had been taken from the ranch for "medical treatment." The Associated Press actually put out a bulletin that Eisenhower was dead, though the bulletin was retracted within a few moments.

Amid growing confusion and near hysteria, Eisenhower's press secretary, James Hagerty, gathered the press together and announced that the "medical emergency" the President had suffered was just a broken cap on one of his teeth; he had been taken to a local dentist to have the cap fixed. Ike appeared in public the next day looking fit and happy, and the incident was forgotten by most. But within the ufological community the rumors continued to swirl.

Palm Springs is not far from Edwards Air Force

Base, where in many versions of the crashed saucer story some of the wreckage and some of the corpses of the flying saucer and crew had been stored. On February 20, 1954, Eisenhower was supposed to have visited the Air Force base to see the evidence firsthand. The rumor continues that Ike had wanted to go public with the information about what he had seen and been told, but that he had been persuaded to remain silent by his military and scientific advisers.

An even more exotic version of this story is that Ike went to Edwards to meet a group of living extraterrestrials who had landed there in five spaceships. The very popular supermarket tabloid the *National Enquirer* reported the tale in an October 1982 article headlined IKE MET SPACE ALIENS. The *Enquirer* based much of its article on the alleged testimony of a former top U.S. test pilot. Eisenhower was said to have asked the aliens to leave Earth so as not to create a panic.

And there is more. An alien given the name EBE 1 — for Extraterrestrial Biological Entity 1 — was said to have survived a UFO crash in 1949 and lived in a "safe house" in Los Alamos, New Mexico, until he died from unknown causes in 1952. There was also supposed to be an EBE 2, who took up residence in the same safe house after 1952. Later an EBE 3 appeared who, according to the rumor, was still alive in the 1980s and may still be alive today.

A major prearranged UFO landing was supposed to have taken place on April 26, 1964, at Holloman Air Force Base in New Mexico. The alien beings came out of their craft and communicated with the waiting crowd of military officials and scientists. If that scene sounds like the climactic scene in the great UFO film *Close Encounters of the Third Kind,* that is not surprising. Steven Spielberg, who is well schooled in UFO fact and lore, is believed to have patterned his scene after reports of the Holloman landing.

One of the persistent rumors in UFO history is that presidents have tried to reveal the truth about UFOs but have always been prevented from doing so by a scandal or other event that distracted and weakened them. In 1973 there was a powerful rumor that the "truth" was to be revealed on an NBC TV special. There were actually supposed to be three shows, then something happened: the Watergate scandal. President Richard Nixon was disgraced and forced to resign. A badly weakened government could not risk such a revelation at a time of crisis. So the truth was not told, and NBC ran only one UFO special.

Before he became President of the United States, Jimmy Carter had been governor of Georgia. While governor, he reported seeing a UFO. On the evening of January 6, 1969, Governor Jimmy Carter was in the small town of Leary, Georgia. At about 7:15 in the evening he was outside the local

Lion's Club waiting to give a speech when he looked up into the sky and saw something he could not identify.

In a later interview he said this about his sighting: "I am convinced that UFOs exist because I have seen one. It was a very peculiar aberration, but about twenty people saw it. . . . It was the darnedest thing I've ever seen. It was big; it was very bright; it changed colors; and was about the size of the moon. We watched it for ten minutes but none of us could figure out what it was. One thing's for sure. I'll never make fun of people who say they've seen unidentified objects in the sky."

After Jimmy Carter was elected President, this incident became famous. UFO critics have said that the future president had actually seen the planet Venus, which under some atmospheric conditions can appear unusually large and bright. It would have been in the sky at about the place where Carter saw his UFO.

Jimmy Carter himself always retained a certain interest in the subject of UFOs, even when he was President.

One of the most interesting connections between presidents and UFOs came in September 1987 when President Ronald Reagan stood before the General Assembly of the United Nations and said that perhaps what the world really needed was a threat from outer space to make the people of the earth forget their differences. Was he hinting at something?

President Reagan had actually made statements like that before. When he met Soviet Premier Mikhail Gorbachev at a summit meeting in Reykjavík, Iceland, in 1986, he talked about a possible invasion from outer space. Gorbachev apparently responded cautiously: "I shall not dispute the hypothesis, although I think it is early to worry about such an intrusion."

Ronald Reagan was known for his offhand, casual, and sometimes careless remarks. But his United Nations speech was not offhand. His UFO statement was part of a carefully prepared text that he read without any ad-libs. Yet when lengthy excerpts from the speech were printed in *The New York Times* the following day, this startling outerspace reference was not included. Was this omission just an accident, or did it reflect a genuine conflict within the government over whether the "truth" should be revealed at this time? This is the sort of question that conspiracy theorists in the ufological community can chew over almost endlessly. Some are convinced that Reagan wanted to reveal the truth but was prevented from doing so by the Iran-Contra scandal that rocked the final years of his administration and greatly weakened his personal power.

The next President, George Bush, was of great

interest to ufologists. Bush had once been director of the CIA, and many saw the CIA as the agency that led the conspiracy of silence. Yet there are rumors that it was ex-CIA chief, former Vice President, and President George Bush himself who was the source of the MJ-12 documents. Like presidents before him, he was trying his best to get the truth out but was prevented from doing so. Or at least so the story goes.

To the best of our knowledge Bill Clinton has never seen a UFO and has no particular interest in the subject — yet.

# CHAPTER FIVE

## The Men in Black

Of all the tales surrounding UFOs, none is more mysterious and frightening than the accounts of the Men in Black.

Right at the start of the Age of Flying Saucers there had been hints about the existence of these sinister figures. A couple of Washington State boatmen claimed that they had seen flying saucers over Maury Island, in Tacoma Bay, early in June 1947. One of the witnesses said that he had been visited by a mysterious man in a black suit who warned him not to discuss what he had seen. It was unclear who this figure was supposed to be, though it certainly sounded as if he were from some government agency, such as the Air Force or the FBI. In 1947 the CIA was brand-new and did not have the fearsome reputation it was to develop in a very few years.

The Maury Island incident was widely regarded as a hoax, so the brief mention of the "man in black" received little attention at the time. But in

1953 the man — or this time Men in Black (the title was always capitalized or abbreviated as MIB) — surfaced once again, all the way across the country in Bridgeport, Connecticut. Ultimately this appearance got a lot of attention.

Albert Bender, a young UFO buff, had formed an organization he called the International Flying Saucer Bureau (IFSB). The organization published a journal, *Space Review*. Despite the grandiose title, the IFSB was only one of many flying saucer groups that had sprung up during that period, and it was not particularly large or influential. The group and the publication were essentially a one-man operation — and that man was Albert Bender.

In 1953 *Space Review* contained this cryptic notice:

"STATEMENT OF IMPORTANCE: The mystery of the flying saucers is no longer a mystery. The source is already known, but any information about this is being withheld by orders from a higher source. We would like to bring the full story in *Space Review*, but because of the nature of the information we are very sorry we have been advised in the negative. We advise those engaged in saucer work to please be very cautious."

The belief that the flying saucer mystery was just about to be solved was widespread among saucer enthusiasts in the early 1950s.

A short time later, Bender suspended publication of *Space Review* and closed up the IFSB.

Some of Bender's friends were puzzled, and they pressed him for details on why he had abandoned the flying saucer field that had so obsessed him. Bender was reticent and evasive. His friend Gray Barker recalled, "Bender had been evasive and close-mouthed about everything except his fear."

But he finally told a sketchy story of being visited by three men in dark suits (later they were inevitably described as men in black suits, the Men in Black, or MIB). He said the trio had been "pretty rough" with him and "not too friendly" and had forced him to get out of "saucer work."

At first Bender's friends were unimpressed by the story. They knew that Bender had been operating his organization and publication on a shoestring. They figured that he had run out of money and found a colorful way of bowing out.

But the story, and particularly the image of the sinister black-clad figures, really resonated in the suspicious and increasingly paranoid world of the UFO buff. Though Bender refused to say anything more about the MIB for years — indeed, he became an almost completely forgotten figure in the UFO world — stories about the Men in Black proliferated.

Albert Bender's original description of his sinister visitors made them sound like government agents from the FBI, Air Force intelligence, the CIA, or enforcers for some powerful but ultrasecret "silence group" within the government. As time went on, the MIB began to take on a far stranger and often unworldly aura.

But earthly or unearthly, the MIB appeared to have one mission — to cover up information on UFO sightings. Anyone who reported a UFO experience, it seemed, might get a visit from these black-clad figures. Actually, Men in Black has become a generic term, for the suspicious individuals don't always have to wear black suits. Often they are impersonating military men in uniform or representatives of other official bodies. But they always have two things in common: They are not who they claim to be, and they are trying to silence or confuse those who seem to know too much about flying saucers. No matter what they are wearing, they are considered Men in Black.

A fairly typical MIB encounter was the one reported by Rex Heflin, a California highway inspector. On August 3, 1965, Heflin said that he took a series of Polaroid pictures of a round, metallic craft hovering over the road near the El Toro Marine Base outside Santa Ana, California. A few days later the photos were published in a California newspaper, and they created quite a sensation. But there were questions about the authenticity of the photographs, and investigators wanted to take a close look at the original shots in the hope of being able to answer some of the questions. Heflin insisted that he had turned the originals over to military men who claimed that they represented the North American Air Defense (NORAD). NORAD officials vigorously protested and said that they had never sent anyone to see Heflin. They didn't even know who he was. The original photos have never surfaced.

But the truly mysterious encounter came two years later. In the early evening of October 11, 1967, Heflin said that he was again visited by men wearing Air Force uniforms. This time Heflin was immediately suspicious. He carefully examined their credentials, which appeared to be in order, and wrote down their names. These new visitors talked about the UFO photos.

During the questioning Heflin said that he noticed a large black car parked across the street. It had indistinct lettering on the front door. According to a report on the incident, "In the back seat could be seen a figure and a violet (not blue) glow, which the witness [Heflin] attributed to instrument dials. He believed he was being photographed or recorded. In the meantime his FM multiplex radio was playing in the living room and during the questioning it made several loud audible pops."

The questions seemed rather pointless, almost random, and the self-described Air Force investigators left abruptly. Once again the Air Force denied that any of its personnel had been sent to question Heflin. It claimed that despite the uniforms and credentials, these men, if they existed at all, were clearly impostors.

Many others reported the arrival of strange visitors in big black cars (usually described as Cadillacs) with peculiar purplish glows inside. Some of the phantom vehicles had a special insignia printed on their doors — a triangle with a bolt of lightning passing through it. Others have said the symbol is the familiar "pyramid with an eye" that is part of the Great Seal of the United States and can be found on the back of a dollar bill. There have been reports of MIB identifying themselves as "agents for the nation of the Third Eye."

Another feature of the cars is that they are always shiny and new. Several people who got close to the black cars recalled that they even smelled new. In the South, shiny new black pickup trucks were reported, and there was even an occasional report of an MIB arriving on a new black motorcycle.

In a typical MIB case, if there is such a thing, the visitors arrive unannounced. Sometimes they arrive at the home of a UFO witness before that witness has been able to report his or her sighting to anyone.

They wear neat black suits, white shirts, and black ties. Some have been described as having slanted or "glowing" eyes, and in other cases they wear wraparound sunglasses, even at night, thus effectively hiding their eyes. MIB are often described as having an olive complexion and being somehow "foreign-looking" or speaking with a strange and unidentifiable accent. They don't seem to be comfortable with the English language. They are either excessively formal and polite or speak as if they had just stepped out of an old Hollywood gangster film: "Look, boy, if you value your life, and your family's, too, don't talk anymore about this sighting of yours."

On October 10, 1966, a pair of teenage boys living in Elizabeth, New Jersey, reported seeing a strange and unearthly being in the woods near their home. The story got some local attention, and it attracted a New Jersey UFO buff named George Smyth. As Smyth was getting ready to question the boys at their home he noticed a large black car parked down the street. Two men got out of the vehicle. The driver stayed in the car. They were all the typical black-suited MIB types. The two men began to ask the boys questions, and Smyth was close enough to overhear part of the conversation. They spoke with an accent he could not identify. The questions were the usual ones about the sighting, but there was a tone in what they said that indicated the boys should not discuss the matter further with anyone else.

Two weeks later Smyth received an eerie phone call at his home. The voice, similar to that of the MIB he had heard, told him to give up UFO investigation altogether. Before he could ask any questions the caller hung up.

UFO researcher John Keel wrote that in a series of investigations on Long Island in 1967 he was told repeatedly of "visits from an Air Force colonel with a pointed face and a dark complexion who demanded that the witnesses remain silent."

Keel also complained that over the years he received ominous and harassing phone calls from unknown persons telling him to drop his investigations. He said that radio and television interviews he had given were mysteriously erased before they could be broadcast, that vital photographs were "lost in the mail," and that on at least two occasions his phone lines were cut. People who claimed to be John Keel or to be working for him appeared at various UFO sites to question witnesses. It was, he indicated, a sinister and troubling series of events.

According to UFO lore, an MIB-type even showed up during the University of Colorado's Air Force–sponsored UFO study. A black limousine appeared in Boulder, Colorado, and a stocky, olive-skinned man wearing a neat black suit and dark glasses stepped out and approached project director Dr. Edward U. Condon. He identified himself as "Mr. Dixsun." He offered to sell the Condon Committee "the secrets of the universe" for a few million dollars. Just exactly what the skeptical Condon made of this is unknown, but no money was forthcoming, so "Mr. Dixsun" got back into his car and drove away. He was never heard from again.

Reports of this sort make the MIB sound strange but human. However, there are many other accounts that make them sound far stranger and more sinister: downright out of this world. Sometimes the MIB seem surprised by ordinary everyday objects like a ballpoint pen or a knife and fork. One witness to a UFO landing in 1966 was visited by a Man in Black. She offered the visitor some Jell-O, and the visitor gratefully accepted. But he didn't seem to know how to eat Jell-O with a spoon. He tried to drink it — without much success.

The movements of the MIB can be stiff and almost mechanical. Take, for example, the odd fellow who visited Dr. Herbert Hopkins in 1976. Dr. Hopkins specialized in hypnotism and was working on a UFO abduction case. He got a phone call from someone who said he was working with a New Jersey UFO group and wanted to talk to him about the case. (Later he discovered that no one from the actual group had ever called him.)

Hopkins agreed to discuss the case, although under normal circumstances he would never have. Less than a minute after he hung up the phone there was a knock at his front door. "I never saw a car," the doctor reported later. "And even if he did have a car he could not have gotten to my house so quickly after making a phone call." Cellular phones were not available in 1976.

The visitor wore the familiar immaculate black suit and tie and gleaming white shirt. "I thought he looked like an undertaker," Hopkins said later. According to the rest of the description, however, the visitor looked more like a corpse. He was completely hairless — bald, without eyebrows or eyelashes. His skin was dead white, and he appeared to be using lipstick.

Amazingly, the doctor let this strange-looking figure into his house. They sat and talked about the abduction case. He told Hopkins to erase the recordings of the hypnotic sessions he was conducting.

At one point the Man in Black asked Hopkins to reach into his own pocket and remove two coins. Hopkins didn't think he had any coins in his pocket, but when he reached in he found that they were there. He was then told to hold one of the coins out in his hand. As the doctor watched, the coin seemed to gradually go out of focus and vanish. "Neither you nor anyone else on this planet will ever see that coin again," the visitor said.

After a while Hopkins noticed that his visitor's speech seemed to be slowing, and his movements were becoming irregular and jerky, like a windup toy that was running down.

The black-clad visitor had trouble getting out of his chair. His parting words were, "My energy is running low. Must go now. Good-bye." He staggered to the door and walked unsteadily down the steps. Hopkins saw a bright bluish light in the driveway, and the visitor was gone. He never heard the sound of a car.

It was only after his guest had literally staggered off into the darkness that Hopkins fully realized how strange his encounter had been. It was almost as though the hypnotist had himself been hypnotized. He was left badly shaken.

Another UFO witness told of the arrival at his house, located at the end of a remote country road, of a tall, painfully thin man wearing a black suit. The visitor did not seem to have arrived in a vehicle of any sort. The man asked all sorts of questions about the UFO sighting, and a host of apparently random and unconnected questions as well.

At one point during the interview one of the visitor's pant legs crept up, exposing part of his leg and what appeared to be a wire running from the top of his sock into the flesh of his calf. As in other cases, this nightmarish figure began "running down" after a while — with speech and movements becoming more and more uncoordinated. At the end of the interview he walked out the door and disappeared.

A classic MIB account was given by a man using the pseudonym "Michael Elliot." One afternoon Elliot was sitting in a university library reading UFO literature when he was approached by a thin, dark-suited man. The man, who spoke with a slight and unidentifiable accent, asked Elliot what he was reading about. Flying saucers, Elliot replied, adding that he had no particular interest in whether they were real or not, just in the stories told about them. The man became very agitated and shouted, "Flying saucers are the most important fact of the century, and you're not interested?!" Then the man stood up "as if mechanically lifted" and spoke gently. "Go well in your purpose," he said and departed. When Elliot tried to follow him he found the library strangely deserted.

Stories of MIB have even transcended the world of UFOs and can be found in other popular mysteries and conspiracies. In the world of Kennedy-assassination conspiracy buffs, there are those who believe that mysterious men in dark suits and dark glasses, as well as black Cadillacs of unknown origin, were observed in and around Dealey Plaza in Dallas, Texas, at about the time President John F. Kennedy was shot.

John Keel, in one of his columns for *Fate* magazine, wrote, "The full story of Kennedy's murder in Dallas in 1963 is filled with incredible details, many of them similar to things found in the most mysterious of the UFO incidents. Photos and physical evidence have vanished or been tampered with just as in so many UFO cases. A widespread assortment of mystery men have been involved. The huge Warren Report [on the Kennedy assassination] contains numerous pieces of sworn testimony describing MIB-type men in the vicinity of Dealey Plaza and the School Book Depository building immediately before and after the assassination."

Here is the sort of incident that sets off waves of excitement in the worlds of assassination buffs and UFO buffs. Fred Crisman, one of the two boatmen involved in the Maury Island incident, was subpoenaed in 1968 to testify before a grand jury in New Orleans that was investigating the Kennedy assassination. This grand jury was convened by New Orleans District Attorney Jim Garrison. It was implied that Crisman was a CIA man or involved in some other kind of undercover work.

Although subpoenaed, Crisman was never called to testify at a trial, and no one knows what, if anything, he said to the grand jury or even if he appeared — but it is just this sort of incident that keeps the UFO conspiracy pot boiling.

David W. Ferrie, one of those Garrison named as a conspirator in the Kennedy assassination (though he was already dead before the accusation was made), had a very vague connection with the ufological world.

Today Garrison's investigation is considered to have been recklessly irresponsible. One man was put on trial as a result of the investigation and immediately acquitted. Still, Garrison's account formed the basis for the extremely popular 1991 Oliver Stone film, *JFK*. Ferrie figures in the film, but UFOs are not mentioned.

Albert Bender, who had really started the whole MIB excitement, kept his mouth shut on the subject for years. Then in 1962 he finally decided to break his silence. He wrote a book called *Flying Saucers and the Three Men* in which he gave more details about his encounter — actually a whole series of encounters — with the strange visitors. They weren't government agents, as his original story made them sound. They were monsters from the planet Kazik. The Men in Black were accompanied by women in tight white uniforms who also had glowing eyes. He wrote of being transported to a secret UFO base in Antarctica.

Bender's book was bizarre and confusing, even in the world of ufology, where the bizarre and confusing are commonplace. The book seemed more like science fiction than a factual account. No one took it seriously. However, the MIB that he first introduced to the world are still with us — more mysterious, more sinister, and more powerful than ever.

They even provided the basis for the most popular summer movie of 1997, called, appropriately enough, *Men in Black*.

# CHAPTER SIX

## The Philadelphia Experiment

On August 15, 1943, a destroyer, the U.S.S. *Eldridge* (in other versions of the story the ship is the U.S.S. *Andrew Fursneth*) literally disappeared from the Philadelphia Naval Shipyard. It was part of a wartime experiment in making U.S. warships invisible that went horribly wrong. When the ship reappeared some hours later, over half the crew was either dead or had gone hopelessly insane. The whole affair was then completely covered up by the authorities.

This strange but compelling story actually entered public consciousness through the UFO world and a man named Maurice K. Jessup. Jessup was an amateur astronomer and one of the early and influential UFO buffs. He wrote several UFO books. His first, *The Case for the UFO*, was published in 1955 and was reasonably popular in the ufological community.

After the publication of his book, Jessup received a series of letters from a man who signed his name Carlos Allende or sometimes Carl M. Allen. The letters were strange, rambling, and almost incoherent documents that hinted at a special knowledge of alien cultures and of UFOs but were often not directly related to space travel and UFOs.

Jessup had called for a test of physicist Albert Einstein's unified field theory, which would bring together apparently disparate theories in physics. Actually, Einstein had never proposed a unified field theory, though some people thought he had. The Allende letters said that the theory had already been tested. Jessup, who like most writers on UFOs received a lot of strange letters, apparently didn't take the Allende letters too seriously at first.

About a year after the publication of *The Case for the UFO* Jessup got a call from the Office of Naval Research (ONR) in Washington. It seems that Allende, or someone else, had sent them a copy of Jessup's book that was heavily annotated in different-colored inks, perhaps by as many as three people. Jessup went to the ONR to discuss this. And here the account begins to turn very murky.

In the most popular and widely repeated version of the story, the officials at the ONR were extremely interested in this publication — so much so that they asked Jessup to allow them to reproduce twenty-five copies of the book with the strange annotations. During the next several years the Navy was supposed to have spent time, money, and a great deal of effort researching the book and the Allende letters. The annotated book had been mailed from Seminole, Texas, one letter from Gainesville, Texas, and another from DuBois, Pennsylvania. Government investigators reportedly searched for the mysterious Carlos Allende but were unable to find him.

From the letters and the annotated book, investigators pieced together a very strange story of a Navy experiment based on the unified field theory that successfully teleported a U.S. warship from its dock in Philadelphia to a dock in the Norfolk–Newport News, Virginia, area and back. The teleportation took only a few minutes. Allende indicated that he had either witnessed the experiment or had gained firsthand knowledge of it. He said that a brief article about it had appeared in a Philadelphia newspaper at the time, but he could not recall the date, so the article could never be located.

According to Allende, the teleportation was only a partial success, because during the experiment half the crew was lost and the other half suffered from bizarre and severe aftereffects. Some, he wrote, were "mad as hatters," while others would "go blank" or "get stuck." He said that they would seem to disappear or "freeze" on the spot. Their positions would be marked, and other members of the crew would walk around the mark.

The annotations to Jessup's book talked about the "mother ship" and "magnetic and gravity fields." Allende seemed to be trying to explain all sorts of mysteries.

Strange and exotic as all of this sounds, it was not unique. People who write about UFOs have become quite familiar with letters of this sort. Many people just toss them in the wastebasket. That may have been Jessup's first reaction. But as time went on, Jessup began to talk more and more about Allende's letters, and his friends became interested in them.

Still, the story of the Allende letters and the Philadelphia Experiment would probably have sunk into oblivion but for one tragic incident. On April 29, 1959, Maurice Jessup was found dead in his car in Dade County, Florida. A hose ran from the tailpipe to the inside of the car, and Jessup had died of carbon monoxide poisoning. He was fifty-nine years old. It was an apparent suicide and did not come as a great surprise to many who had known Jessup. He was a troubled and increasingly depressed man who had often talked of suicide.

But in the conspiracy-filled UFO world a rumor began to spread almost immediately that Jessup had not killed himself but had been murdered and his death made to look like suicide. He was killed, the talk went, because he knew too much. But there was never any agreement on who the assassins were or what Jessup knew.

Jessup's death suddenly made the Philadelphia Experiment and the Allende material significant in the UFO world. Various versions of the story have been written up regularly in UFO publications, and it even became the basis for a 1986 movie, *The Philadelphia Experiment*, and for an episode of *The X-Files* first aired in 1995.

The passage of time has simply deepened the confusion surrounding the whole incident. From the very start, the Navy declared that the whole thing was a hoax and that there had never been any official interest in Allende's material. However, official spokesmen did admit that some individuals in the Department of the Navy had been interested and that they had privately printed up the copy of Jessup's book with the Allende annotations and letters.

Of course, there are those who insist that it is all a cover-up, that the Navy knows all about the Philadelphia Experiment but that the file on it is so secret that it will never be released. One researcher even claimed that the mysterious Allende file was completely destroyed in an equally mysterious fire.

Then there is the identity of the mysterious Carlos Allende himself. Perhaps Navy investigators were never able to find him, perhaps they never looked, but a man claiming to be Carlos Allende showed up at the headquarters of the pro-UFO Aerial Phenomena Research Organization (APRO). He told the group that the whole thing had been a hoax and that he had written the letters because "Jessup's book scared me." However, he did make some strange comments hinting he knew a great deal about UFOs that he wasn't willing to talk about. Later he tried to take back his "confession."

There have been a number of people claiming to be the real Carlos Allende. Many believe the real Allende is actually named Carl M. Allen — a name that "Allende" sometimes used. Allen was born in Pennsylvania in 1925 and has corresponded for years with UFO buffs and others who have an interest in the strange and mysterious. By all accounts, Allen is a genuinely odd fellow who has spent a lifetime moving from one motel to another. His family has claimed that he made up the whole Philadelphia Experiment story.

Some have speculated that the entire idea of the Philadephia Experiment began with experiments in degaussing — the neutralizing of a ship's magnetism so that it can pass over magnetic mines without setting them off. A degaussed ship, in a sense, disappears — but only magnetically; the physical body of the ship stays just where it is. Perhaps Allen had heard about this possibility and had become confused.

But in the minds of many this sort of mundane speculation is all just part of the cover-up. The February 1997 edition of *Fate* magazine, the nation's number-one purveyor of information on UFOs and other strange subjects, contained a special section on the Philadephia Experiment.

In one article, writer Patrick S. Carbone says that the Philadelphia Experiment was an attempt to cloak the ship in an electromagnetic field so that it would not be detectable on radar. However, the experiment went horribly wrong, trapping those on board "in the middle of what may be considered the world's first and possibly largest microwave oven."

The survivors would have been treated in military hospitals under the strictest secrecy. To cover its tracks, the government itself released disinformation. "It concocted stories about invisibility, teleportation, and men set adrift in space and time. The fantastic tales may have been inspired by the actual ravings of the survivors whose brains had been damaged by the intense electromagnetic waves," the article said.

Carbone believes that the tales were designed to hide the awful truth and make the Philadelphia Experiment "just another old sea tale similar to the Flying Dutchman."

But the very same section of the magazine contains what is certainly the most fantastic tale yet. It is written by someone who calls himself only "Drue."

Drue claims to be a survivor of the Philadelphia Experiment — sort of. The experiment, he says, was not merely meant to test invisibility, magnetic or otherwise, or even teleportation. It was a scientific experiment to explore the space/time continuum. And there was more, what he calls an "extraterrestrial agenda."

"Extraterrestrials, working with government officials, wanted to map the earth's magnetic gridwork for interdimensional travel."

And there was even more — an attempt to rewrite history:

"Think about the immense power one could have by moving instantly from one event in time to another. Power is what motivated those behind the scenes to conduct the Philadelphia Experiment."

But as in all the other accounts of the Philadelphia Experiment, something — perhaps everything — went wrong. The ship that Drue calls the U.S.S. *Eldridge* was sent hopping through time and space. It is supposed to have appeared briefly at Sebago Lake in Maine in 1997 and will reappear at Imperial Reservoir in California in 2005.

Most of those who had been aboard the *Eldridge* died horribly during the hop through time. Drue was one of the survivors, but he had received doses of radiation that were slowly killing him. So he agreed to take part in another experiment. This time his spirit was sent forward in time to the year 1962 and moved into the body of a boy who was dying. But the scientists who did this also erased his memories of his past existence and most specifically of the Philadelphia Experiment.

The boy containing Drue's spirit grew up, joined the Marines, served twenty-two years, and retired.

But shortly before his retirement strange memories and flashbacks began to surface of his past life and of the Philadelphia Experiment. He now spends his time researching the subject.

Now that sounds like yet another *X-Files* plot, and perhaps someday it will be.

Clearly this is not a tale that needs to be taken seriously. It is just another example, though a remarkably fantastic one, of the persistence of belief in the Philadelphia Experiment. And remember where it all started, with somebody scribbling in the margins of a UFO book.

# CHAPTER SEVEN

**Conspiracy Theory**

Sometimes it seems as if nothing is as it seems. The country is awash is conspiracy theories.

People believe President Kennedy was killed by the CIA, the Cubans, or the Mafia. Take your pick. Unless they were all working together with the help of the MIB.

There are theories that the federal building in Oklahoma City was bombed by agents of the U.S. government in order to create hysteria that will result in repressive gun laws being passed by Congress.

Some think that mysterious black helicopters, part of a secret United Nations force poised to take over the United States, have been spraying poison over farmers' fields and harassing U.S. citizens.

Others believe that AIDS is an artificially created disease that has been deliberately spread throughout the world by the CIA.

These theories and many more are widely circulated in pamphlets, newsletters, magazines, and newspapers, on radio talk shows, by videotape and audiotape, and, increasingly, through the Internet.

Belief in a variety of exotic conspiracy theories is nothing new to America. In the 1950s a lot of people in the U.S. believed that putting fluoride in the water supply to reduce tooth cavities was part of a Communist plot to soften the will of the American people to resist aggression. But conspiracy theories are now more numerous and exotic than ever, spread more quickly, and have more believers.

In the view of writer and conspiracy fan Jim Hougan there are two types of history available: " 'the safe, sanitized version,' so widely available as to be unavoidable . . . and a second one that remains secret, buried, and unnamed."

Authors and conspiracy buffs Jonathan Vankin and John Whalen give this second version of history a name. They call it conspiracy theory. Conspiracy theory, they say, is an antidote to the "*New York Times* version" or the "TV news version" or the "college textbook version" of history.

"The main resistance to conspiracy theories comes not from the people on the street but from the media, academia, and government — people who manage the national and global economy of information."

In short, they contend, there is a conspiracy to keep you from hearing about the conspiracy theories.

There is probably no subject in recent history

that has been more associated with conspiracy theories than UFOs. It would be useful to look at a few of them.

## UFOs ARE NAZI INVENTIONS

Among the unexplained aerial phenomena that predated the flying saucer era were the "foo fighters" of World War II. During the closing months of the war, pilots on some Allied planes reported that they had been followed, even "teased," by glowing balls of light while on missions over Europe. Similar experiences were reported by U.S. pilots in the Pacific theater as well. The objects were undetected by radar and never seemed to do any harm, but the sightings were too numerous to be dismissed as imaginary.

These glowing balls were dubbed "kraut balls" or more popularly "foo fighters." The name came from a once-popular comic strip about a fireman named Smoky Stover. A line often repeated in the strip was "Where there's foo there's fire."

Immediately after the war the foo fighters were all but forgotten in the glow of victory. But when flying saucer accounts began to multiply in mid-1947 they were recalled and have since been regarded as being related to the UFO phenomena.

Some pilots who encountered the foo fighters believed that they might have been some sort of German secret weapon that had been designed to confuse pilots or radar. Allied intelligence examined German records after the war but found no evidence of experiments with anything like the foo fighters. The "mystery" of the foo fighters was never really solved. The generally accepted explanation is that they were reflections of light on the planes' wings or some sort of glowing electrical plasma phenomena.

Not so, proclaimed Italian aircraft engineer and writer Renato Vesco. In a 1969 article in a popular American magazine, *True*, Vesco said Allied investigators had really discovered a wealth of secret Nazi work on remote-controlled *Feurbälle* or fireballs. "Fast and remote-controlled, the fireballs, equipped with kliston tubes and operating on the same frequency as Allied radar, could eliminate the blips from the screens and remain practically invisible to ground control."

And that's just the start. Other researchers suggest that the little foo fighters were merely prototypes of much larger round craft the Nazi scientists were working on. According to one confidential Italian document, there had been an aerial dogfight between Allied planes and a remarkable vehicle. "A strange flying machine, hemispherical or at any rate circular in shape, attacked them at a fantastic speed, destroying them within a few seconds and without using any guns."

UFO researcher Timothy Good and others believe that after the fall of the Nazi regime some of the scientists and engineers who had developed the

Nazi "flying saucers" then went to work secretly either for the United States or the Soviet Union to further develop the craft. A lot of German rocket scientists did, in fact, do exactly that. But Nazi flying saucer scientists remain in the realm of conspiracy theory.

Conspiracy theorist Jim Keith has written that German scientist Rudolph Schriever said that "the various UFO reports since the end of the war showed that his Kugelblitz designs had been discovered and put into production."

The theory that flying saucers were really secret U.S. craft based on German designs had a brief popularity in the early 1950s, but it has pretty much died out today.

However, even stranger theories are still around — *much* stranger theories. Vladimir Terziski insists that, in the final days of the Third Reich, leading Nazis — including possibly Hitler himself — escaped to the South Pole aboard U-boats and UFOs. There they established an underground New Berlin, which now contains some two million inhabitants. Nazi flying saucers regularly emerge from this underground world to terrify and puzzle the supposedly victorious peoples who live on the surface of the earth. Is it any coincidence that flying saucers first appeared in 1947 — after the destruction of the Nazi regime? According to this theory, it isn't.

## SECRET GOVERNMENT CONSPIRACY

The belief that the U.S. is run by a "secret government" is a popular one. It was probably inevitable that UFOs would figure into this belief.

The most prominent purveyors of the UFO secret government theory were John Lear, a pilot who said he once flew for the CIA, and Milton William Cooper, a retired Navy officer. They were leaders in what was called the "dark side movement."

In general, the "dark siders" say that the world is controlled by a ruthless secret government. Among its other activities, this secret government runs the international drug trade and has released the artificially produced AIDS virus and other deadly diseases on the world as a means of population control. The ultimate goal is to turn Earth and surrounding planets into slave-labor camps. They are going to do this with the help of space aliens with whom they have been in regular contact.

## THE OUTER LIMITS

In the realm of UFO conspiracy theories it is difficult to determine where or what the outer limits might be. But what has been called the ultraterrestrial theory — or the Grand Deception — must come close to those limits.

What has most frustrated UFO buffs over the

last half century is the elusiveness of the space aliens — their apparent unwillingness to communicate directly and openly, to land in some obvious place like New York's Central Park, or to leave behind some unambiguous piece of physical evidence.

To the conspiracy theorist, the reason is that all the information is being covered up by a conspiracy of silence. Still, that is not an entirely satisfactory explanation. Even vast conspiracies make mistakes, information leaks out, someone talks, something is found. And the aliens themselves could easily blow the whole conspiracy away by actually landing in Central Park.

But what if the deception is being carried out by the aliens themselves? What if they are deliberately creating the uncertainty and confusion for reasons that we cannot begin to fathom? And, moreover, what if these aliens are not little green men from Mars or little gray men from Alpha Centauri but beings from another dimension, another reality, a different but parallel universe? Then, of course, the puzzling behavior and the lack of conclusive evidence make perfect sense — sort of.

The popular UFO theorist Jacques Vallée proposed what has been called the control system theory. He says that UFOs are part of a system that has been used throughout human history to condition human behavior. "I have not yet determined whether it is natural or spontaneous," says Vallée, "whether it is explainable in terms of genetics, of social psychology, or of ordinary phenomena — or if it is artificial in nature and under the power of some superhuman will."

Vallée believes that one of the things UFOs have brought about is a change in the public attitude toward the possibility of extraterrestrial life. Slowly, he says, we are being brought around to a greater acceptance of the idea.

"My assumption," says Vallée, "is that a level of control of society exists which is the regulator of man's development. I am also led to the assumption that the action of UFOs operates at this level. What does this explain? First, it explains why there is not contact. Direct contact would ruin the experiment . . . it would preclude genuine learning."

John Keel, a prolific writer of ufological topics, tosses off highly speculative theories with great abandon. In his book *UFOs: Operation Trojan Horse*, Keel proposes that the UFO intelligences are not merely extraterrestrials but "ultraterrestrials" — entities from unimaginable other dimensions. And they are probably hostile. Human beings, says Keel, are "like ants, trying to view reality with very limited perceptive equipment. . . . We are biochemical robots helplessly controlled by forces that can scramble our brains, destroy our memories, and use us in any way they see fit. They have been doing it to us forever."

Another of his theories is that a senile supercomputer left over from an ancient age produces psychic manifestations such as ghosts and monsters to prevent us from finding its physical location. UFOs are just another one of these manifestations.

All of this speculation is mind-boggling and ultimately mind-numbing. If a half century and more of UFO excitement is only an illusion created by beings whose very existence we are unable to comprehend or control, or if they mislead us for reasons that are utterly beyond our understanding — what can we do? From this perspective UFOs can be anything, everything, or nothing.

We can't disprove it, but we can't prove it, either. We can't understand it, and we certainly can't do anything about it. The only reasonable conclusion one can come to is — to forget it.

The ultraterrestrial theories have enjoyed a certain vogue among hard-core UFO buffs, but as most of us begin to read them over, in a short time our attention starts to wander, our eyelids become heavy, and the book slips from our fingers as we drift off to sleep.

The truly far-out theories are hypnotic but not, one suspects, in the way their creators wished them to be.

# CHAPTER EIGHT

Area 51

For many years the center of the mystery was the Wright-Patterson Air Force Base near Dayton, Ohio. That was where Air Force intelligence was centered. That's where the alien bodies from the Roswell crash were stored in Hangar 18. That's where the secret files from Project Blue Book were stored.

Now it's a place in Nevada called alternately Nellis Air Force Base, Papoose Lake, Groom Lake, the Box, Red Square, Water Town, Dreamland (an acronym for Data Repository Establishment and Management Land), or, most commonly, Area 51.

Area 51 is a large complex of military facilities, all of them extremely secret. It is located in the dusty Nevada desert about eighty miles (130 kilometers) north, northwest of Las Vegas. It's the sort of remote spot in which the government likes to test weapons.

Publicly, the government will not say what is going on in Area 51. In fact, the government has in the past even denied that there really is such a facility, a rather foolish thing to do since some of the structures can actually be seen from the surrounding hills, and UFO buffs hold regular vigils in the area to watch what they believe to be alien craft zipping over the landscape.

Area 51 is now unquestionably the most well-known secret facility in the world. Granted, it's off the beaten path. Area 51 is not marked on official maps. The closest road is a desolate ninety-two-mile (154-kilometer) stretch of Nevada State Route 375 that runs through the scrub country. But in 1997 the promotion-minded Nevada highway executives officially named the road the "Extraterrestrial Highway." It has become a tourist attraction. How's that for secrecy?

The biggest town on the Extraterrestrial Highway is Rachel, Nevada. It is little more than a trailer park, a gas station, and a diner. It has a population of about one hundred. When the tourists come, and they do come in increasing numbers, they are sure to stop off at the Little A'le Inn, now the most famous roadhouse in Nevada. It is a restaurant-motel-gift shop that sells items such as Extrater-restrial Highway doormats and playing cards. Outside the inn there is a drawing of a space alien with a large, bald head shaped like an inverted pear, huge, slanting eyes, and a slitlike mouth. It is the image of a space alien that has become most familiar today. Another sign on the inn proclaims EARTHLINGS WELCOME.

The fame of the not-very-secret Area 51 has grown enormously in recent years. The outskirts of the facility are visited regularly by TV crews filming news shows or documentaries. A live television discussion on UFOs and the UFO cover-up, hosted by Larry King, was held in the desert near Area 51.

Tourists can buy Area 51 caps, T-shirts, and other memorabilia in the town of Rachel and from a number of mail-order companies. If Area 51 was supposed to have been secret, it has turned out to be the worst-kept secret in history.

But just knowing that it is there does not tell you what goes on inside Area 51. The government most certainly won't say. Though the curious have gathered around the perimeter of Area 51, casual visitors are strictly forbidden inside, and there are no guided tours. There are fences and guards and some of the most up-to-date security equipment available anywhere in the world. This includes ground-motion detectors, heat sensors, and high-powered infrared telescopes. There are antennae that can detect vehicles in motion twenty-five miles (forty-two kilometers) away. The security patrols are reportedly recruited from elite military units like the Green Berets and Navy SEALS. Visitors who want to get a closer look than the guards think they should are likely to be arrested. The guards are not fooling around. It all looks and sounds like it came out of a science-fiction movie or an episode of *The X-Files*.

There is no doubt that secret activity — a lot of it — goes on behind the high-tech defenses and heavily armed guards in Area 51. Aside from military personnel there are thousands of civilian employees. Many of them are flown into Area 51 from a restricted airport in Las Vegas. Most of the civilian employees work for EG&G, one of the nation's largest defense contractors. They work on short-term contracts, generally for about three months in very restricted areas. Like most employees who work with highly classified material, the employees at Area 51 are required to sign statements that they will not reveal the nature of their work. Inevitably some have talked, but since the scope of an individual's work is usually restricted, they haven't been able to reveal much about what is actually being built and tested.

A few who claim to be former Area 51 workers, however, have said they know a great deal more about what is going on. The problem is that the stories they have told are often contradictory.

But in most accounts, 1947 appears to be the key year. That is the year that EG&G was started. It is the year that the CIA was formed. And, of course, it is the year that the modern era of flying saucers began.

Many of the stories that are told about Area 51

link it to the alleged flying saucer crash at Roswell, New Mexico, in July 1947. According to these theories, government investigators not only recovered the bodies of space aliens but a good deal of advanced alien technology as well. There was an immediate but secret rush to try to understand this technology and adapt it for earthly use. Remember the Cold War and the confrontation with the Soviet Union? Whichever nation got hold of the secrets of this advanced technology first would have an enormous advantage over the other. We wanted to get the technology before they did.

*The Day After Roswell: The UFO Cover-up*, a sensational book published in June 1997, contends that Air Force investigators not only found a downed alien craft in July 1947 but began a huge secret program to use technology contained in the wreckage. The author of the book, retired Army Lieutenant Colonel Philip Corso, says that he personally headed the project that distributed alien technology, such as lasers, computer chips, and fiber optics, throughout the U.S. economy and particularly in the military establishment. The aim, according to the book, was to help America get ready for an inevitable alien invasion. The alien technology also helped the U.S. win the Cold War.

Lieutenant Colonel Corso had served as an aide to Senator Strom Thurmond, chairman of the Senate Armed Services Committee. Corso's book contains a foreword by Senator Thurmond, who praises his former aide as a man of integrity. However, Thurmond insists that he didn't know anything about the UFO stories in the book when he wrote the foreword. "I did not, and would not, pen the foreword to a book about or containing a suggestion that the success of the United States in the Cold War is attributable to technology found on a crashed UFO," said the senator.

*The Washington Post* commented, "Hmmmmm. Maybe Agent Mulder can get to the bottom of this."

The general feeling is that the material from the Roswell crash was taken first to Wright-Patterson Air Force Base near Dayton, Ohio, and later transferred to the more remote and secure Area 51. There appears to be no general agreement as to when this transfer took place.

The UFOs that have been seen so frequently over the area are in reality ships made here on Earth using alien technology. But some suggestions go a great deal further than that. In a 1997 television special on Area 51, a man claiming to be a former employee of the secret facility said that he was not only working with alien technology, but that he was actually working under the supervision of a space alien! One of the familiar big-headed, gray-skinned, bug-eyed variety. The man said that he had been "authorized" to give out that information and that great public revelations about the alien-directed activity in Area 51 would be made "soon."

Unfortunately, the real name of the informant was not given, and he was shown only in silhouette so there would be no chance of identifying him. To date, the promised revelations have not been made. Anyone familiar with the history of ufology is depressingly familiar with anonymous revelations of this sort. Time passes and nothing is revealed.

Some of the speculation about what goes on in Area 51 has turned what might be called conventional UFO thinking on its head.

Former Regional Director of the Civilian Intelligence Network and Area 51 researcher Norio Hayakawa says that the whole idea of extraterrestrial visitations is a deception carried out by the U.S. government to gain control over its citizens, you and me!

In this view there never was a flying saucer crash at Roswell. It was staged by the government. The real technology for advanced saucer-shaped craft was captured from the Nazis at the end of World War II and developed by the government in super-secret facilities such as Area 51. The Roswell crash is just a fabricated cover story.

Another theory claims that Area 51 is developing microchips that will be implanted secretly in the cards issued to every U.S. citizen as part of a national health plan. These chips will allow people to be tracked by an array of over eight hundred secret satellites. The technology is so advanced that a satellite can photograph your fingerprints, eavesdrop on your conversations, and shut down your automobile, without you knowing it.

All of the information gathered is funneled to Area 51, where gigantic secret files on everyone are stored. That is what the name Data Repository Establishment and Management Land really means.

Some of the most vigilant believers in a government cover-up think that the alien abductions that have been reported are not really being carried out by space aliens but by the federal government. They are part of a CIA experiment to gain control over the entire population. The space aliens are a cover story to hide the inhuman and illegal activities of earthly agencies.

All of these theories make you wonder which is worse, the government or the aliens.

You can hear all this sort of speculation — and a lot more — down at the Little A'le Inn in Rachel, Nevada, where earthlings are still welcome.

# CHAPTER NINE

Fifty Years and Counting

In April 1997 thirty-nine members of a UFO cult called Heaven's Gate killed themselves in a rented mansion in southern California. Videotapes made before the mass suicide indicated that members of the group believed that the Hale-Bopp comet, which was just then becoming visible, was accompanied by a spaceship and that this was a signal that they were to be taken up "to the next level." In one form or another this particular group had been in existence for over twenty years. They had wandered the country like nomads, waiting for a UFO to arrive and, as one of the members put it, "beam them up." Apparently they got tired of waiting and decided that suicide was a way to hasten their departure. By all accounts the members of the Heaven's Gate cult were educated, intelligent, and generally good people.

No one knows how many groups there are in the country whose beliefs center around UFOs — probably hundreds. Very few are ever driven to anywhere near the extremes of Heaven's Gate. But just because their beliefs seem strange, bizarre, and even crazy to the rest of us, we should not underestimate the strength of these beliefs.

In June 1996 three members of a UFO group on Long Island, New York, were indicted for planning to assassinate county political leaders. Apparently they had become convinced that forest fires on Long Island had been caused by the crash of a UFO and that this was being covered up by federal authorities and local police. The leader of the UFO group got the idea that the police were trying to kill him for exposing the cover-up. He was going to protect himself by killing the political leaders and taking over the local government.

All of this extraordinary testimony confirms that many Americans believe in UFOs, some to a deadly extent.

I was introduced to flying saucers as a science-fiction-reading kid in 1947. I followed the subject with avid interest for years. Along with most other buffs I was convinced that the "truth," whatever it was, would be revealed "soon." There seemed to be one deadline after another. But nothing big ever happened.

As I grew older, while I never lost my interest, I became disillusioned. Eventually I decided that the day of the flying saucer was done. In 1966 I wrote a nice little nostalgic piece called "Whatever Happened to Flying Saucers?" I lamented the passing of the good old days of the 1950s when people really "believed" in flying saucers. Fortunately some editor changed the title of the article before it was published, because boy, was I ever wrong. The year 1966 marked the start of one of the regular periodic upsurges of interest in UFOs.

Since then I have tactfully refrained from predicting the end of interest in the subject.

As recently as the fall of 1997 there have been stories about possible evidence of microscopic life on Mars, conditions favorable for the existence of life on one of the moons of Jupiter, even organic chemicals in the Hale-Bopp comet. Suddenly the possibility of other life in the universe looks a lot brighter than it did just a few years ago.

Of course, none of that means that the life is advanced, intelligent, and interested in visiting us in round spaceships — but it makes one wonder.

And what about the cover-up, the conspiracy of silence? Just follow the news, and there are regular revelations about what the CIA knew but never told about nerve gas in Iraq or what the FBI knew about illegal campaign contributions from China. Now that's a very great distance from suspecting a half-century-long cover-up of evidence of extraterrestrial visitations. But it all adds to the general feeling of distrust of the authorities — the feeling that they know a lot of things they are not telling us. In the summer of 1997 an article by CIA historian Gerald K. Haines was made public. The article revealed that in the 1950s and 1960s the Air Force had deliberately misled the public about a huge number of UFO sightings. People were seeing tests of secret U.S. aircraft, and the Air Force wanted the tests to remain secret. It was what many of us had suspected but not known in detail.

Even without the big revelation that I hoped for, the atmosphere seems right for a continued interest in UFOs. You're certainly interested, or you wouldn't have read this book in the first place.

I'll just leave you with the final line from one of my very favorite UFO films — *The Thing* (1951). I first saw the film when I was around fifteen years old and fascinated by flying saucers. The words are:

"Keep watching the skies!"